10 Stories to Make a Difference is a collection of ten original illustrated stories for young readers, all inspired by the theme of *difference*. The collection features a mix of well-known and emerging writers and illustrators, giving a platform to untold stories and diverse new voices. Produced by Pop Up Projects, a non-profit, UK-based national children's literature development agency, 10 Stories celebrates Pop Up's 10th birthday in 2021. Proceeds from sales supports Pop Up's work in deprived schools, marginalised communities, and with talented writers and illustrators, especially from backgrounds that are under-represented in children's publishing. 10 Stories will be an annual publishing event, with a whole new collection planned for 2022.

Find out more at **www.pop-up.org.uk**

Laura Dockrill is a writer and illustrator whose books for children include *Darcy Burdock*, *Sequin & Stitch* (with Sarah Ogilvie), *Angry Cookie* (with Maria Karipidou), and YA novels *Lorali* and *Big Bones*. She's been shortlisted for Waterstones Book of the Year and longlisted for the Carnegie Medal. Laura's work for stage and screen include the BAFTA-nominated *Goldfish*, the children's play *Dust* for Half Moon Theatre, and commissions by The National Theatre, Young Vic and Donmar Warehouse.

Ria Dastidar is an illustrator and designer from London who loves dreaming up colourful, surreal, and funny characters: cuddly monsters, confused rabbits, and apples that remember the good ol' days. She's an illustration mentee on Pop Up's Pathways into Children's Publishing programme (2019-2021). *Magnificent!* is Ria's first published children's book.

Edited by **Emily Ball**, Flying Eye Books
Art directed & designed by **Lilly Gottwald**, Flying Eye Books

Publisher **Dylan Calder**
Coordinator **Amanda Saakwa-Mante**
Designer **Txabi Jones**

MaGnIficeNT!

Written by
Laura Dockrill

Illustrated by
Ria Dastidar

Sometimes I forget that I'm different –
it's an easy mistake to make.

I mirror myself on everyone else,
because everyone acts the same.

But I have strange thoughts too, you know?
I struggle with fears and doubts.
I don't always like the same things others do,
but I don't want to feel left out.

I get confused too, you know?
I get muddled up and lost.
And when I'm shy, my mouth dries up,
and my cheeks get horribly hot.

I try my best to join in,
but I overthink, worry and erase.

And when things go wrong, I hide how I feel,
and pretend everything is ok.

Because I know how it feels to be the new kid,
when nobody knows your name.

When the world moves like a school of silver fish,
and to blend in seems like the only way.

That's why it stuck out when I met you,
I was reminded how it feels to be strange.
Like a bandaged-up thumb, or a hard math sum;
out of time, out of date, out of place.

But it was only a flip of the coin today,
that made you the new kid, not me.
Tomorrow you could be looking for a hand in the dark...
I hope it's mine that you see.

Yes, same is safe, same is free,
same is cosy, comfy and easy.

But same is boring, a waste of time.
Same is a game of cheating!

"THANK FUDGE!"

We are all different: snowflakes, trees,
creatures of the wild.

"IT'S GREAT!"
We are all different,
like the fingerprints of a child.

So today I join in with someone else,
someone who is different too.
Someone who has other ideas and dreams –
who teaches me something new.

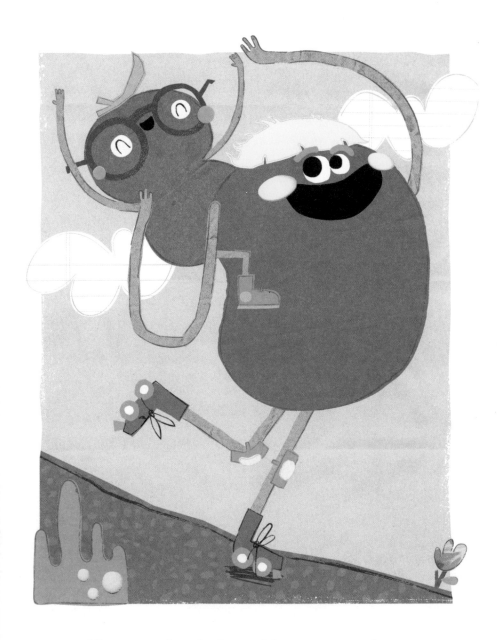

The next day I play with someone else,
someone who flaps their arms like wings.
Someone who likes that, not this!
Who likes a bunch of other cool things.

After that I talk to another friend –
one that I only made just now.
This someone was born in a whole other town,
yet we skip in the same playground.

Then I halve my sandwich with a kid,
who is a bit younger than me.
Because bread is bread, and that is it.
Now neither of us is hungry.

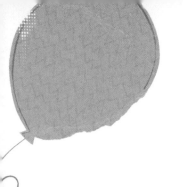

Then finally I catch the eye,
of that new kid I met days ago.
And I remember how it feels to be different,
in fact, it's something I'll always know.

Because being different is being alive!
It's not a failure or an accident.
So why don't you join your smile up with mine...

To Bob and Buzz (Laura)

For my family, Mum, Dad and Rishi (Ria)

Thank You!

The 10 Stories collection has been made possible through the generosity and love poured into these stories by our old friends and new, the writers and illustrators who all gave their wisdom and magic: Philip Ardagh, Avital Balwit, Jamie Beard, Sita Brahmachari, Eleanor Cullen, Danica Da Silva Pereira, Ria Dastidar, Alexis Deacon, Laura Dockrill, Jamila Gavin, Sahar Haghgoo, Jay Hulme, Daniel Ido, Krista M. Lambert, Jane Ray, Jacinta Read, Chris Riddell, David Roberts, Marcus Sedgwick, Anjali Tiwari. And through the kindness and devotion of the brilliant publishing editors, art directors and designers who volunteered their time to transform these great stories into even greater books: Emily Ball, Liz Bankes, Andrew Biscomb, Jane Buckley, Alice Curry, Holly Fulbrook, Lilly Gottwald, Elorine Grant, Libby Hamilton, Daisy Jellicoe, Txabi Jones, Ruth Knowles, Tiffany Leeson, Jacqui McDonough, Caroline Royds, Chloé Tartinville, Holly Tonks, Clare Whitston, Sean Williams. Huge gratitude to Matt Baxter and Lydia Fisher at Baxter & Bailey for donating their time to produce the 10 Stories brand, style and formats. If it wasn't for the 643 donors to our crowdfunding campaign, these books may never have made it to print - and we especially want to thank Rachel Denwood and Simon & Schuster, Sam Arthur and Nobrow, Michelle McLeod and Baillie Gifford, the CSR team at Linklaters LLP, Tim Bevan, Wolfgang Tillmans and all our former Board members for their generous support. Behind the scenes, the team and Board at Pop Up kept this great ship afloat through these most turbulent times, and we cannot thank them enough for always being part of the story no matter how hard the story gets.

Made possible by